The Night of His Birth

KATHERINE PATERSON

The Night
of His
Birth

Illustrated by Lisa Aisato

flyaway
books

Sing out, my soul, the wonder . . .

They are gone now, those shepherds, smelling of their sheep and rubbing their faces with chapped and grimy hands, eyes still dazed with angel light.

"Please, can we touch him?" Their hands reached toward the child my arms held close.

How could I say no? God is the host of this strange celebration at which I am also a guest.

Like these rough men, I, too, was startled by an angel. "Hail, most favored one!" he said. And through his messenger, God summoned me, as though to play a divine joke on a prideful world. Pity Isaiah. When that noble prophet sang of David's coming son, could he have dreamed of me?

Not even my mother could do that. When I returned so full of joy from Elizabeth's house, she met me with angry tears. She could not believe the good news my swelling body bore. My own mother— who once held me, just as I hold this child of mine.

My father did not speak, but I could see the questions in his eyes. Does she lie? Has she gone mad? And which is better, there being no comfort in either answer? They are sick with shame, for they are simple, pious people who care what the neighbors say.

Even Joseph doubted—but how could
I blame him? An angel come to Nazareth?
God's Holy Spirit come to me, a nothing
child, a poor man's girl? King David's
mighty shout shrunk to a whisper in our
peasant blood?

But God is good. Joseph had his own
stern visitor. And though my man sang
no magnificat, he did obey. God give him
joy for that.

And there he sits, meaning to keep
watch, his head a stone upon his chest.
Not knowing—he trusts. My heart
swelled to feel his pain, his puzzlement,
and then, tonight, I saw the gentle way
he washed the son God gave into his care.

The boy stirs in his sleep. I have fed him, and he is satisfied. Can you believe it? God's anointed one upon my breast, with milk, just there, at the corner of his tiny mouth.

His hair is black and thick and stands
up like weeds upon his head. I try to
smooth it with my lips, but it springs back,
refusing my correction. I laugh aloud.

My Joseph moans. I have disturbed his
rest, but how can I be silent? Every part
of me shouts and sings. I have brought a
child into the world. From my own flesh
has come this perfect thing.

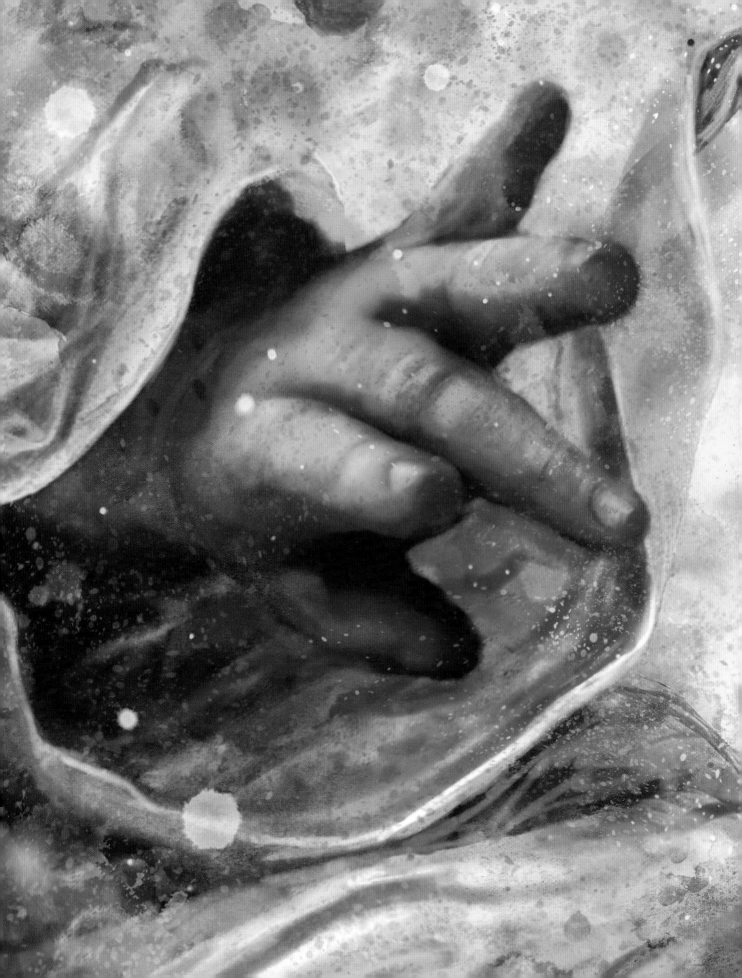

A little hand pokes through the bands. Unpracticed as I am, I have not wrapped him well; he moves within the cloths to nestle into the curve of my body. We are almost one again. But now I can see him. I can touch him. I can nurse him and care for him.

He is God's. I know that. I heard the word of angels in my cousin's cry of praise; I saw it in the rough fingers of the shepherds smoothing this downy cheek in wordless worship.

He is God's, and God's ways are past all
my understanding. I cannot see the man he
will become, or even the ruddy-cheeked boy.
I do not know what God will ask of him—
or me. I am the handmaid of the Lord; my son,
his servant. Dare I say? My son, God's son.

But now, this morning, the light breaks.
The world wakes to a day that has never
been, and I hold my baby in my arms, and
that alone is miracle beyond belief.

*S*ing out, my soul, the wonder . . .

For Jennifer, with gratitude and love from all the Patersons

—K. P.

Text © 2019 Minna Murra, Inc.
Illustrations © 2019 Lisa Aisato

Adapted from a story first published in *The Presbyterian Survey*, December 1985

First edition
Published by Flyaway Books
Louisville, Kentucky

19 20 21 22 23 24 25 26 27 28–10 9 8 7 6 5 4 3 2 1

Book design by Allison Taylor
Text set in P22 Stickley Pro

Library of Congress Cataloging-in-Publication Data
Names: Paterson, Katherine, author. | Aisato, Lisa, illustrator.
Title: The night of his birth / Katherine Paterson ; illustrated by Lisa
   Aisato.
Description: First edition. | Louisville, Kentucky : Flyaway Books, [2019] |
   "Adapted from a story first published in The Presbyterian Survey,
   December 1985." | Summary: After the shepherds leave and while Joseph sleeps,
   Mary holds her baby boy, Jesus, rejoicing and marveling over her role in his
   nativity.
Identifiers: LCCN 2019001547 (print) | LCCN 2019002597 (ebook) | ISBN
   9781611649567 (ebk.) | ISBN 9781947888128 (alk. paper)
Subjects: LCSH: Mary, Blessed Virgin, Saint--Juvenile fiction. | Jesus
   Christ--Nativity--Juvenile fiction. | CYAC: Mary, Blessed Virgin,
   Saint--Fiction. | Jesus Christ--Nativity--Fiction.
Classification: LCC PZ7.P273 (ebook) | LCC PZ7.P273 Ni 2019 (print) | DDC
   [E]--dc23
LC record available at https://lccn.loc.gov/2019001547

PRINTED IN CHINA

Most Flyaway Books are available at special quantity discounts when purchased in bulk by corporations, organizations, and special-interest groups. For more information, please e-mail SpecialSales@flyawaybooks.com.